D0064956

Discarded
_____ Co. Public Libr____

Family for Sale

Also by Eth Clifford

The Dastardly Murder of Dirty Pete
Flatfoot Fox and the Case of the Bashful Beaver
Flatfoot Fox and the Case of the Missing Eye
Flatfoot Fox and the Case of the Missing Whoooo
Flatfoot Fox and the Case of the Nosy Otter
Harvey's Horrible Snake Disaster
Harvey's Marvelous Monkey Mystery
Harvey's Mystifying Raccoon Mix-up
Help! I'm a Prisoner in the Library
I Hate Your Guts, Ben Brooster
Just Tell Me When We're Dead!
The Man Who Sang in the Dark
Never Hit a Ghost with a Baseball Bat
The Remembering Box
The Rocking Chair Rebellion
Scared Silly
The Summer of the Dancing Horse
Will Somebody Please Marry My Sister?

Family for Sale

ETH CLIFFORD

Houghton Mifflin Company
Boston   New York   1996

BLUE GRASS REGIONAL LIBRARY
COLUMBIA, TENNESSEE 38401

Copyright © 1996 by Eth Clifford Rosenberg

All rights reserved. For information about permission
to reproduce selections from this book, write to Permissions,
Houghton Mifflin Company, 215 Park Avenue South,
New York, New York 10003.

For information about this and other Houghton Mifflin trade
and reference books and multimedia products, visit
The Bookstore at Houghton Mifflin on the World Wide Web
at http://www.hmco.com/trade/.

Manufactured in the United States of America
Book design by Celia Chetham
The text of this book is set in 13 pt. New Baskerville
BP   10   9   8   7   6   5   4   3   2   1

Library of Congress Cataloging-in-Publication Data
Clifford, Eth, 1915 –
Family for Sale / Eth Clifford
p.   cm.
Summary: When their mother goes away
for two weeks, five siblings take turns being in charge.
ISBN 0-395-73571-8
[1. Family life — Fiction.   2. Brothers and sisters —
Fiction.   3. Responsibility — Fiction.]   I. Title
PZ7.C62214Fam   1996   94-40957
[Fic] — dc20   CIP   AC

For David,
because

Contents

1. Meet Sherm the Worm 1
2. Rob the Slob 11
3. Tillie the Terrible Tyrant 19
4. The New Boss 29
5. From the Frying Pan into the Fire 35
6. Over My Dead Body 46
7. Where's Sherm? 53
8. Pete's Plan 63
9. If It's Broken, Don't Nix It 71
10. Family for Sale? 81
11. The Lucky Sign 90

Family for Sale

1

Meet Sherm the Worm

Sherm the Worm was thinking about his family.

He sat in a chair in his room and thought.

He sat on his bed and thought.

He sat on the floor and thought some more.

Then he told his dog Tip, "I hate Rob. I hate him to pieces."

Tip wagged his tail. He was a big dog, so there was a lot of tail to wag. Anything Sherm said to him, Tip agreed with at once. He especially agreed about Rob.

"Yip, yip, yip," Tip yowled.

Sherm understood dog language. He knew Tip was telling him that Rob was his least favorite human, too.

There was no doubt that Rob was a trouble-maker.

Last night, in the dining room, when Tillie, their oldest sister, asked Rob to help their brother Pete clear the table, he refused. He put his thumbs in his ears and wiggled his fingers at her. Tillie's eyes grew stormy. Then he poured ketchup in Sherm's milk and said, "Hey, Sherm. There's blood in your milk. That's a bad omen."

Trudy, the second oldest sister, threw her napkin down, then punched Rob's arm. "You're disgusting," she told him.

"You wouldn't act this way if Mom was here," brother Pete said.

"So? When is she here anyway?" Rob said.

It was true that their mother, Libby Evers, was out of the house most of the time. She worked as a waitress during the day. At night she went to school hoping a better education would lead to a promising career and a good salary.

"You want her to quit her job?" Pete asked. He shook his head. "How dumb can you get?"

"She didn't have to go away on a two-week cruise," Rob shot back.

Libby Evers had won the cruise in a radio slogan contest. She had been undecided about going until Tillie convinced her she needed to be by herself for a while. She did seem very happy to go off, away from the telephone, the daily grind, and, Rob firmly believed, her kids. Before she left, she told them, "I'm leaving Tillie in charge. You guys better listen to her, hear?"

"We promise," they said, all except Rob. Now he sat at the table, determined to give Tillie a hard time.

Suddenly Tillie sniffed. "Rob! I can smell you from across the table. Never mind clearing up. Go take a bath."

"What for?"

"I just told you. You smell."

"So? What do you expect? You get smelly doing pushups and running and — "

Tillie pushed her chair back. "You want me to put you into the tub?" she asked sweetly.

You had to watch out when Tillie was sweet. Rob knew that. He knew she would get Trudy and Pete and even Sherm to help drag him to the bathroom. It wouldn't take much for Tillie to become furious enough to get into the tub with him and scrub his bones until they were squeaky clean.

"You know what you are?" Rob shouted. "A tyrant, that's what. A really terrible tyrant."

Sherm grinned now, just remembering last night.

"And you know what, Tip?" Sherm stroked him behind his ears, then Tip tried to lick Sherm's face with his long tongue.

"She called him Rob the Slob. So Rob got back at her and gave us names, too. He called Trudy the Moody, and Pete the Neat. And you know what he called me?"

Tip waited for the answer, although he probably knew it. At least his bark sounded as if Tip knew.

"That's right. He called me Sherm the Worm. I'm not a worm. I'm not."

He got up from the floor and stretched out on his bed, which delighted Tip, who made himself comfortable next to Sherm.

Tillie wouldn't have liked that at all. She always tried to discourage Tip from sleeping on Sherm's bed. She made it clear to Sherm that Tip was not to share his pillow at night. Tip paid no attention, of course. Why sleep on the floor, Tip figured, when it was so much cozier nestling next to Sherm?

But Tillie didn't fuss too much. She understood that when you were eight years old, small for your age, and afraid of your own shadow, it helped to have a big dog handy.

Besides, this huge old house they lived in was scary, especially at night, when it was full of creaks and unexplained noises. It didn't help when every once in a while the wind howled outside and whistled its way inside.

This house was once owned by a rich old lady who hadn't minded living in a three-story house with lots of rooms in it, rooms with fancy names — the study, for example, and the sewing room, and the upstairs parlor, to name just a few. There was even an apartment over the garage for the live-in chauffeur. Grandpa Marsh lived there now.

Sherm's mom and dad had bought the house "for a song." That meant they were able to buy it for very little money. His dad thought he could turn it into a boarding house, but nothing ever came of that idea. Nothing seemed to come of most of Dad's ideas.

Sherm sat up again. It was hard to think lying down, and he wanted to think about the names Rob gave them all.

You couldn't tell, just by looking at Tillie, that she was a Terrible Tyrant, because she was just your normal, everyday teenager, with their mom's straight black hair and sky-blue eyes. Rob always said that Tillie, who was quite slender, looked as if a high wind could snap her in two. But she had an iron will, as everyone in the family knew. She had to be strong-minded, because she did run the family. Mom depended on Tillie. And of course Tillie was practically all grown up. She was seventeen, going on eighteen any day now.

"You know what, Tip?" Sherm asked.

Tip wagged his tail to show he was listening.

"Rob is right about Trudy. She really is moody."

Sherm thought about that for a while. Trudy was fifteen, going on sixteen, but not very soon. She was quite different from Tillie. Trudy had curly blonde hair, deep brown eyes, and a mouth that drooped at the corners.

Trudy daydreamed a lot, which was why she forgot to do chores around the house. She often told her family that someday she would be a famous rock singer, though she had a voice like a broken foghorn. Or she would be a fabulous movie star. People would push and shove each other just to catch sight of her. She would live in a mansion . . . Trudy would get lost in her dreams until someone, usually Rob, shook her out of them. Then she would turn sulky and moody, and nibble at her nails. Rob didn't care. He liked teasing Trudy.

Whenever Mrs. Evers caught Rob at it, she would scold him. "Girls of fifteen have a right to be moody. They have a right to daydream, too. So stop annoying your sister. It's hard enough to be fifteen without someone pestering you. Find something useful to do," she would add.

"Like what?" Rob always asked, although he knew the answer because Mom said it often enough.

"Go clean up your room. For starters," Mrs. Evers would snap.

"What for? It'll only get messed up again."

"I don't have time for this, Rob." Mrs. Evers always said that, too. "Why can't you be more like your brother Pete?"

"Be like *Pete?* You're kidding, right?"

Pete was eleven, and didn't look like any

other member of the family. His hair was so fair it seemed almost white. His eyes were large and mismatched, one blue, the other hazel. He was almost as tall as Rob, which didn't please Rob at all, since he was two years older. As far as Rob was concerned, the worst thing about Pete was that he was neat and orderly.

Nothing in Pete's room was ever out of place. Like Rob, he had a desk in his room. But Pete arranged his schoolbooks in careful piles on the left side of his desk. Notebooks were in the top drawer, precisely marked. A divider kept his pens and pencils and markers in separate compartments. He even wore pajamas when he went to bed!

Downstairs, Pete always straightened the living room, no matter how often he had to do it. Sometimes he straightened the chair when you got up, even if you planned to sit right down again. In the dining room, Pete cleared the dishes as soon as everyone finished eating, and sometimes before. He often stood behind Rob and snatched his plate away because he couldn't stand the sloppy way Rob ate.

Even Tillie sometimes lost patience with Pete.

Several times she wondered, "I don't know who Pete takes after in this family."

Rob had an answer for that. "He's not really part of this family."

When the others stared at him, Rob went on, "You know what probably happened? They gave Mom the wrong baby to take home from the hospital."

"Now I've heard everything," Tillie said.

"Wait a minute," Rob argued. "Take a good long look at him. You know anybody else here who has hair and eyes like his?"

"That's the most ridiculous thing I've ever heard," Tillie snapped.

"Pete *is* different," Trudy said. She stared at him as if she had never seen him before.

Did this bother Pete? He just looked at everyone around the table, then he studied Rob, who was grinning. "Okay," he said finally. "You tell me where my real family is and I'll be packed in ten minutes."

Sherm sighed. He was tired of thinking about his family. He wished there was a small switch, an invisible one of course, that he could use to turn off his mind when he was tired of thinking.

He grinned. Maybe he'd be an inventor some-day . . .

"Uh, oh," he told Tip. "I must be daydreaming, just like Trudy."

Tip barked. That meant he was getting restless.

"You know what, Tip? Let's go down to the kitchen and get some chocolate milk. And cookies."

Tip began to run around in circles. Some words were a signal to him — words like kitchen. And cookies. He raced out of the room and down the steps, stopping only once to look back.

"You go ahead," Sherm said. "I'll catch up to you."

If Sherm had known what would happen next, he would have stayed in his room.

2

Rob the Slob

Tip had better luck than Sherm. He whizzed past Rob, who was seated at the dining room table, working at a model airplane. Tip made it safely to the kitchen. Meanwhile Rob checked to see if he had all the materials he needed. Then he frowned as he realized he wouldn't have enough glue and string.

He glanced up just in time to see Sherm tip-toeing into the kitchen. Rob nodded his head and grinned.

"Hey Sherm, you little worm," he ordered. "Run upstairs and get me my glue and string."

Sherm wanted to say, "NO!" He longed to reply, "Go get it yourself."

He knew better than that, though. Rob was thirteen, and he was big, and rough, and mean.

"Well," Rob said impatiently. "Are your feet stuck to the floor? Get going. I need that stuff now."

Sherm shrugged, then left the dining room to go upstairs. A puzzled Tip followed. Sherm could almost hear Tip asking, "What happened to the cookies and the chocolate milk?"

As they went up the steps, Sherm told Tip. "I'll make believe this is a treasure hunt."

Of course it would be a treasure hunt, because Rob would never have put the glue and string in a logical place, like his desk. Before he opened the door, Sherm took a deep breath. Tip backed away, his tail between his legs.

Tip and Sherm knew what to expect. They had been in Rob's room before. Sherm told himself, "Maybe this time I'll be lucky. Maybe this time I can just go in and get out before I have to take another breath."

He turned and tried pleading with Tip. "Come on. Dogs are hunters. You can probably find the glue and string . . ."

Tip growled, stretched out on the landing, and buried his head between his paws.

"Scaredy-cat," Sherm said. On his way into the room, he shoved a trail of dirty paper plates, broken plastic cups, and squashed sodapop cans to one side. He pushed a torn, tattletale gray sheet, a pillow with wisps of feathers poking out, and a moldy, half-eaten hamburger with onions off the bed.

Of course the glue wasn't there. No string, either.

Sherm glanced around and sighed. Their mom had threatened Rob, had punished him, had even stopped talking to him, had read books on what to do with a child like Rob.

"If only your father was here," she would sometimes murmur.

But Mr. Evers wasn't there, hadn't been for a long time, not since Sherm was four. Of course, they had Grandpa Marsh, but that wasn't like having a real father.

Sherm sighed again. Where should he look now?

He crouched down to peer under the bed, then shook his head. No way would he put his hand in there. Not even a mouse would be foolish enough to work its way through that jumble. Then he spotted the bones.

Tip's bones! No wonder poor Tip walked around with a puzzled look, wondering why and how they always seemed to vanish.

Sherm leaped to his feet. He stamped them hard on the floor. "You're mean! You're dirty rotten mean!" he shouted. He hoped Rob could hear him through the floors. "You've been stealing all of Tip's bones. If I was Tip, I'd bite *your* bones."

He was so furious he decided not to search for the glue and string after all. But then he spotted them, half-hidden under a pair of blue jeans in a corner of the room.

Tip sprang up when Sherm came out of Rob's room at last, but Sherm paid no attention to him. He raced down the steps, burst into the dining room, threw the glue and string on the table, and shouted, "I'm never going into your room again. Not even if you kill me and cut me up into a million pieces."

Tip looked up at Rob and growled.

Rob just laughed.

14

"Come on, Tip," Sherm said. "Let's get out of here."

Tip seemed surprised that Sherm had forgotten the cookies and chocolate milk, but he followed him faithfully. Sherm was headed for the garage to find his grandfather.

Grandpa Marsh was the only member of the family Sherm liked. He really cared about you. He let you talk, and he listened to every word you said. Tillie was always too busy; Trudy never wanted to be bothered; Pete said Sherm shouldn't expect others to fight his battles for him. And Mom was forever tired.

Sherm loved to visit with Grandpa Marsh in the garage. Grandpa Marsh used half of it as his workshop. The nice thing about Grandpa was that most of the time he didn't mind being interrupted.

"Well! Look who's here," he would say, sounding real pleased.

Or, when he saw the expression on your face, he would ask, "Is it time for us to talk, Sherm?"

Or he would look at you, grin, and say, "I just closed my eyes this minute and made a wish.

Know what I wished? That you would pop in and keep me company."

Now that he was retired, Grandpa Marsh carved wooden toys of all kinds. Mostly he favored circus figures — lions, tigers, monkeys, elephants, acrobats, clowns . . .

He shaped, sawed, smoothed, scraped, painted, and polished each toy. When he was done, he placed them all in a large cardboard box. Then he wheeled the box in a cart to Children's Hospital, three blocks away. There he visited the children and gave away the toys.

Grandpa Marsh didn't usually encourage talking when he worked. So, while he was busy, Sherm began to think again.

Forgetting Grandpa Marsh's rule, Sherm said suddenly, "I don't like Tillie and I don't like Trudy and I don't like Pete. They always let Rob pick on me. That's mean. I'm only a little kid. They're supposed to take care of me."

Grandpa Marsh held up his finger, then put it across his lips. "Hold on one second, Sherm," he said.

Sherm thought about Rob some more. How could Rob sleep in a room that looked as if it

16

had been hit by a tornado? Whenever Mom saw it, she sighed and called it a disaster.

Rob was a scowler and a scruncher. He scowled so hard, his eyebrows seemed to meet. Sometimes Tillie would tell him impatiently, "It's not against the law to smile once in a while, you know."

"If he ever smiled, his lips would crack," Trudy would always add.

His scrunching was what seemed to bother Mrs. Evers most. She was forever saying, "Rob, will you for heaven's sake straighten up? If you keep on scrunching the way you do, you'll wind up shaped like a crooked U."

Sherm sighed. It was a long, sad sigh that captured Grandpa Marsh's attention at once. He put down the tiger he had just begun to polish and said, "All right, Sherm. Out with it. What's bothering you?"

"It's Rob . . ."

Grandpa Marsh shook his head. "Again? Or still?"

"Still." Sherm bit his lower lip. "Can I tell you something? You won't get mad at me or anything?"

"I won't get mad. That's a promise."

Sherm took a deep breath and said in a rush, the words tumbling out as if he could no longer hold them back, "I don't want Rob to be my brother anymore."

Tip, who had been fast asleep all this time, woke up and growled. He liked dozing in the garage whenever Sherm and Grandpa Marsh spoke to each other. But when Sherm said he didn't want Rob to be his brother anymore, his voice had become loud and shrill.

Sherm stroked Tip's head, and he lowered his voice, but he repeated, "I mean it, Grandpa. I really mean it."

Grandpa Marsh didn't blink an eye. He didn't even look surprised. He just said quietly, "I know exactly how you feel, Sherm. Your brother can be hard to live with at times."

"Not *at* times," Sherm said. "All the time."

3

Tillie the Terrible Tyrant

Grandpa Marsh had put down the tiger when Sherm began to talk. Now he picked it up again, along with a polishing cloth, but Sherm interrupted him once more.

"You think, if my dad was here, he would let Rob act so mean?"

"I honestly can't say, Sherm. Your did didn't always notice what was going on around him."

Sherm was surprised. "He didn't? How come?"

"Your dad's mind was always busy with some new scheme on how to get rich quick."

"Like buying our house?" Sherm knew all about that. Every once in a while, his mom would say it might not be a bad idea to try to sell it. But all the kids protested. Sell the house?

Where would they go? They loved living here. They would go on and on until Mrs. Evers would agree it would never be put up for sale.

"Like the house," Grandpa Marsh agreed. "When the boarding house plan didn't work out, he decided to buy a restaurant." Grandpa Marsh didn't tell Sherm that Dan Evers had borrowed the money from him and lost it all.

"After that, he came up with all kinds of other ideas, but nothing worked out. He got real restless. When he was here, he wanted to be there. When he was there, he had to try someplace else. The last time he left, he just walked out and never came back."

"My friend Richard has two fathers. I bet if I had two fathers, Rob would have to be extra nice to me."

Tip had heard enough conversation. He was hungry. Couldn't Sherm remember chocolate milk and cookies? How long was Tip supposed to wait?

When Tip began to pace, Grandpa Marsh laughed. "I know that growl. You'd think Tip can tell time. He certainly has an instinct for when the next meal is due. Tell you what,

Sherm? Why don't I put this tiger aside, wash up, and then let's go over to the house." He looked at his watch. "Yep. It's suppertime. Tip always gets it right."

After Grandpa Marsh had washed and changed into clean clothes (paint and varnish sometimes stained the old pants he wore in the garage), they walked to the house. Tip raced ahead, turning now and then to make sure he was being followed.

When they entered the dining room, all the others were already there. Pete and Trudy were setting the table; Tillie was in the kitchen putting food into various dishes. Rob had scrunched down in his seat, giving directions. No one paid any attention to him.

"Sit down, Grandpa," Tillie said as she came out of the kitchen with a tray. "We're just getting ready for supper."

Rob sat up. "I don't smell anything." He sniffed hard. "I thought we were going to have pizza tonight."

"There won't be any junk food while I'm in charge," Tillie told him. Their mom was in the habit of serving fast foods. When she came home from work, she had no time to spare before she had to go off to school. Tillie understood, but this was her opportunity to get healthful foods into the family.

She sat at the foot of the table — Grandpa Marsh was at the head — and lifted the cover off the tray.

Rob stared, then shook his head. "I can't believe this," he said. "Where's the food? I mean the real food?"

"Right under your nose," Tillie answered impatiently.

Rob shook his head again, harder. "Come on. This isn't for real. This is stuff you feed rabbits."

"Really? I'll have you know that the most popular area in a restaurant is the salad bar. Salads are healthful. They're tasty. They're good for you —"

That was when Trudy interrupted. "I hate foods that are good for me. Whey can't we have fried chicken? And mashed potatoes with gobs of gravy? And doughnuts and muffins? And —"

"Yeah. Or hamburgers. What's the matter with hamburgers? And sour pickles? And french fries?" Rob demanded.

"You always want hamburgers," Pete said. "You'd eat hamburgers for breakfast. Why can't we have Chinese —"

"I don't want Chinese," Sherm said. "Why can't we ever have peanut butter and jelly sandwiches?"

Tip barked.

"See?" Sherm said. "Tip wants peanut butter and jelly, too. Don't you, Tip?"

"What's that dog doing in here?" Rob shouted. "Get out of here, Tip. Go eat your dog food."

Tip began to slink out of the dining room. At the kitchen door, he stopped and sent a woeful look at Sherm.

"He is not a dog." Sherm was furious. "He's my friend. He's my best friend in the whole world. He doesn't want dog food. He doesn't even like dog food. He can have half my peanut butter and jelly sandwich."

"Hey, guys," Grandpa Marsh said. "You're not giving this food a chance. Tillie went to a lot of trouble — "

"Who cares?" Rob interrupted, then stopped short when Tillie slammed a fist down on the table. Along with her dark hair and sky-blue eyes, Tillie had fair skin that reddened when she was angry. And she was very angry now.

"You all listen up." She shot a furious glance at them. "You're all spoiled rotten. I'm sick of your complaints. I don't care what you like. I'm trying to keep you all healthy. But you're too dumb to realize that. Well, while I'm in charge, you'll eat what I tell you to, and —"

When Tip heard the edge in her voice, he slid under Sherm's chair, or at least as much of him as he could squeeze in.

Rob turned to Grandpa Marsh. "She's not in charge, Grandpa. You are. Tell her. Go ahead, tell her."

Grandpa Marsh's head went back and forth.

"There's no use asking me to interfere, Rob. Your mom put Tillie in charge while she's away. You know that. You all know that."

"It's not fair. Mom doesn't know what a terrible tyrant Tillie is."

"Yeah," Trudy added, glaring at her sister. "A tyrant who thinks she runs the whole world."

"But that's what tyrants do," Pete explained. "Tyrants always make decisions nobody likes."

"Well, tyrants get overthrown all the time," Trudy pointed out.

Grandpa Marsh thought it was time to rescue Tillie, who looked as if she was about to explode.

"You kids aren't being fair to your sister. She's the oldest child, the one who looks after all of you when your mom isn't here. She has to make the decisions. Even if you don't like them. But don't forget, you've all felt free to express your opinions. That's what you can do in a democracy."

"Yes," Pete agreed. "But in a democracy you get to vote for somebody you want to run things."

"A family is not a democracy," Tillie declared. "Parents are always telling their kids what they can do and what they can't do. When the parent isn't around, then the oldest person in the family takes over. And I'm the oldest. So I'm the boss."

"Grandpa is the oldest," Pete corrected. He was very good at correcting people. He did it all the time.

"No," Grandpa Marsh said. "I don't live with you."

"You practically do," Sherm pointed out.

"No. I have my own little apartment over the garage. That's my little kingdom. When I come here, I'm a guest."

Sherm thought that was strange and said so. Grandpa Marsh just smiled.

"Well, is this discussion over now?" Tillie wondered. "Now you've all had your say, you better dig in and eat before I clear the table."

She helped herself to a selection of salads, then put three large crackers on her plate.

"Those crackers look as if they're made out of straw and pasteboard," Trudy muttered.

"NO!" Rob folded his arms and glared. He was fed up. That was how he put it. "I'm fed up. Up to here." He pulled his finger across his throat. "You're not going to push me around anymore!"

For once Trudy agreed with him. "Rob is right. I don't care if Mom did tell you to take over. She isn't here and we are."

"We don't need you, Tillie. I could run things around here with one hand tied behind my back," Rob announced.

"So could I," Trudy agreed.

Grandpa Marsh rapped his knuckles sharply on the table. "All right. I've heard enough. Maybe each one of you *should* take turns running things. Learn what it is to be responsible for a family's needs and wants."

"I just want a peanut butter and jelly sandwich," Sherm said.

Rob turned and studied his grandfather. His eyes gleamed. "You mean it? You really mean we can each take turns being the boss?" He rubbed his hands together. "When do I start?"

"You don't."

Rob started to protest, but the look in Grandpa Marsh's eyes stopped him. Nobody argued with him when his eyes turned that frosty, not even Libby Evers.

"If Tillie agrees," Grandpa Marsh said after a moment, "and *only* if Tillie agrees, everyone will have a chance, in order of age."

They waited to see if Tillie objected.

Tillie sat with her arms folded, but she didn't say a word.

"I'm next in age." Trudy was delighted. Her smile almost reached from ear to ear.

Rob didn't give up easily. "It isn't fair. It was my idea."

"Don't you ever give up?" Pete asked impatiently. "Grandpa *is* being fair. You expect anybody to listen to you, you'd better wait your turn."

Rob was about to say something more, but changed his mind. "Okay. But I come after Trudy, and don't you forget it."

Tillie laughed.

"What's so funny?" Sherm asked. "Aren't you mad you can't be the boss anymore?"

"No, Sherm. I'm not mad." She turned to the others. "Go ahead. Do what you like. Maybe you'll all learn something the hard way. Anyway, now I can start thinking of myself for a change."

Trudy immediately objected. "They can't do what they want. I'm the new boss now, and everybody has to do what I say. You too, Tillie."

Tillie grinned.

"Welcome the new tyrant, folks," she said.

4

The New Boss

"First announcement," Trudy said. "We're going to have some real food in this house for a change."

"Great!" Rob rubbed his hands together. "Now we get hamburgers."

"No," Pete said, "Chinese."

Trudy gave them a frosty glance. "I'm the new boss. We eat what I say. Fried chicken. With all the trimmings. Tillie can go get it right now, because she's the only one who can drive. And no arguments from anybody."

Sherm whispered to Tip, "Never mind about the peanut butter and jelly. You'll like the chicken."

Tip wagged his tail in agreement. He would have eaten peanut butter and jelly — Tip would eat almost anything — but chicken was more to his taste.

Tillie stared at Trudy for a long moment, then shrugged and pushed back her chair. In a moment, they heard the front door slam shut. Tillie had agreed to a new boss, but she didn't have to like her decision.

Trudy sighed. It was a sigh of deep satisfaction. What a wonderful feeling to be in command, to make people do what you wanted them to do, whether they liked it or not.

"Now. Here's the rest of the plan," Trudy told them. "After supper, we'll watch television."

Rob agreed immediately. "Suits me."

"Wait a minute. What about our homework?" Pete never had to be reminded to do his homework. He *liked* doing homework. He took great pleasure in how it looked when he was finished. If he made a mistake and had to erase a word or two, he tore up the sheet and began with a new one. Nobody else in Pete's classes ever handed in such neat homework assignments.

"You can do it after we watch TV," Trudy began, but Pete shook his head. "Listen, Trudy, you never stop watching."

"I do no such thing," Trudy said. But it was true.

Trudy was fascinated with horror movies and science fiction stories. The more horrible they were — the scarier, the bloodier — the more spellbound she was. She didn't have to worry she'd run out of programs. If there weren't any on TV, which was unlikely, she could always play a film on the VCR.

Sherm spoke up suddenly.

"Pete is right. He shouldn't have to watch TV if he doesn't want to. I don't want to, either. You always turn on programs where people get killed and there's lots of blood and screaming. Or else there are giant spiders that eat people, or tomatoes that swallow houses, or aliens that are giant skeletons, or —"

"Don't be such a child," Trudy said.

" . . . or mad scientists who kidnap you and turn your brain to mush," Sherm went on.

"That's what happened to Trudy," Rob said. "A mad scientist has already turned her brain to mush."

"No wonder Sherm has nightmares," Pete said.

"It's not my fault he's such a baby," Trudy insisted. "He knows it's all just make-believe."

Grandpa Marsh decided it was time to give a word of advice. "Sherm has a good point there, Trudy. You should keep in mind that he's only eight."

Trudy's lips tightened. "Bosses can't worry about things like that," she told him.

"You're forgetting the whole idea," Pete reminded Trudy. "Grandpa thought we should find out how to take on responsibility."

"I sent Tillie for real food, didn't I?" Trudy argued. She looked at Grandpa Marsh, then looked away. Then she glanced at Sherm, whose face was a study in misery.

"Okay," she agreed. "I'll let everybody do what they want to after supper."

Pete winked at Grandpa Marsh, who winked back.

Sherm sighed with relief.

"That doesn't mean that I'm not going to look at my programs," Trudy warned. "It just means nobody has to watch unless they want to."

Grandpa Marsh sent Trudy an approving

32

smile. "I think Sherm and I would like to play checkers. And at bedtime, I'll read a book to Sherm. Or he can read one to me, right, Sherm?"

Before long, Tillie came in with several cartons that gave off a wonderful fragrance.

"Food! Real food!" Trudy was responsible for the family getting a tasty meal at last.

No one spoke again for a few minutes. Everyone was too busy eating, even Tillie. When Trudy shot her a triumphant glance, Tillie explained, "If this is all I'm going to get, of course I'm going to dig in. I'm starved."

"It isn't Chinese," Pete said, between mouthfuls. "But I'm not going to starve myself either."

Pete was always prepared to be reasonable, except when it came to orderliness.

After supper, Tillie spoke to Trudy privately as they stacked the dishes in the dishwasher.

"Listen, Trudy, it's really not as easy as it sounds, taking care of the family. There are so many things you have to be responsible for —"

"Like what?" Trudy interrupted.

"Like making sure everyone takes a shower before bedtime. Especially Rob. And getting up early enough in the morning to wake everyone in time so they won't be late for school —"

"I know all that. You don't have to tell me. You're just trying to show me what a tough job you have, right?"

"It's not that at all, Trudy," Tillie tried to explain.

"You sure think a lot of yourself, Tillie. What's the big deal, anyway? Well, I'm the new boss now. I'll show you all," Trudy said, and flounced out of the room.

Tillie looked after her and shook her head.

"What's up?" Pete asked. He had just popped into the kitchen to make sure it had been left spotless.

"What's up?" Tillie responded. "I'll tell you what's up. I smell disaster, with a capital D."

5

From the Frying Pan into the Fire

Tillie was right. Trudy's turn was a disaster. With a capital D.

Everyone at the table the next evening was furious.

"I don't care what anybody says," Rob started, before anyone else could speak. "Trudy does have mush where her brain should be."

He folded his arms and glared at Trudy. She glared back. "Who asked you for your opinion?" she wanted to know. "Anyway, I'm running things now, and you have nothing to say about it."

"Well, I have a lot to say." Pete usually spoke in a quiet voice, but not now. He startled everyone; he was actually yelling.

"Me, too," Sherm chimed in. When Tip barked and ran around in circles, Sherm added, "And Tip also."

Tillie was silent. All she did was lean back in her chair, raise one eyebrow, and let a small smile curl her lips.

Soon they were all talking at once. That was the moment Grandpa Marsh put his fingers to his lips and blew a shrill whistle that left them with their mouths open. Grandpa Marsh had never done that before. It took them completely by surprise.

"All right," he said, when there was silence. "Let's go about this situation logically." He turned to Trudy. "As you can see, we have rebellion in the ranks."

"What's rebellion?" Sherm asked. He didn't know what it meant, but he sure liked the sound of it, especially since Trudy seemed to hate it.

Rob scowled. It didn't bother Trudy, who didn't care how Rob looked. But it made Sherm nervous. That was how Rob's face seemed most dangerous. That was when Rob thought up some new way to torment Sherm.

36

"Rebellion," Pete explained, "is planning to get rid of somebody who rules over you."

"Especially tyrants," Rob said.

Sherm was puzzled. "I thought Tillie was the Terrible Tyrant." Then he clapped his hand over his mouth.

But Tillie didn't seem to mind. She just grinned.

"Tillie was overthrown in the first rebellion," Pete explained.

Sherm studied his brother. He still didn't like Pete, but he had to admire him for being really smart.

How did he do it? How was Pete able to know so many different things, even stuff he never learned in school? True, Pete read a lot. He always seemed to have a book in his hand. Still, how did he keep all that information inside his head?

Sherm closed his eyes for a moment. He didn't want to think about anything else right now because he was very upset with Trudy. He turned to her now and accused, "You didn't wake us up this morning."

"So?"

"So we all overslept."

"Big deal." Trudy shrugged. She began to bite away at one of her fingernails. She always did this when she knew she was wrong. "So what?"

"I'll tell you so what." Pete broke in, furious. "It meant we didn't have time for breakfast. And then we all missed the school bus. And Tillie had to drive us to school, so she was late."

Tillie agreed. "That was your responsibility, Trudy. That is what being boss is all about. Responsibilities. All kinds of responsibilities."

"I hate missing breakfast," Pete went on.

He was as orderly about meals as he was about everything else. You arose at a certain time, you had breakfast at a certain time, and then you went to school, definitely at a certain time.

This morning he had arrived in class too late for the math quiz. Pete was a whiz at math quizzes. Missing this one spoiled his whole day, even though he received an A+ on his English test.

"And Mrs. Hailey told me she was very provoked when I came in late," Sherm announced. "She said I disrupted the whole class. What's disrupted —"

"Do you have to know what everything means?" Rob asked.

Sherm was too busy complaining to pay attention to his brother.

"Then she said again she was provoked, real loud, right in front of everybody. And they all laughed. What's provoked?"

"Provoked is what we are now at Trudy." Pete glared at his sister. "Double and triple provoked."

Rob glanced up at the ceiling and rolled his eyes. "How do you expect Sherm to know what you're saying? Provoked is spitting mad."

Sherm was shocked. "Teachers don't spit."

Rob groaned. "I can't talk to this kid."

"Can we eat now and argue later? I don't know about you, but I'm starved." Trudy turned to Tillie. "Did you get everything?"

"What's everything?" Rob was suspicious. "You didn't even ask us what we want tonight."

He didn't have to wait for long. Tillie

went into the kitchen and came back with . . .

"Chicken? Fried chicken again?" Pete couldn't believe this was happening. "We had chicken last night."

"So?" Trudy speared a chicken breast with her fork, then scooped up some mashed potatoes, over which she poured half the gravy.

"I hate this stuff," Rob said. But Sherm noticed it didn't stop Rob from putting plenty of food on his plate.

Sherm crossed his arms. He looked down, pushed his lips out, and got ready to cry.

"I don't like you, Trudy," he said after a while. "You're not a nice person."

"You're breaking my heart." Trudy bit into a corn muffin, which crumbled part in and part out of her mouth.

"Tillie," Sherm said. "Can't you tell Trudy —"

Tillie held up her hand as if she was stopping traffic. "Don't complain to me. You all thought I was Tillie the Terrible Tyrant, remember?"

Sherm turned to Grandpa Marsh. "Grandpa, did we elect Trudy?"

40

"In a manner of speaking."

What did Grandpa Marsh's answer mean? Was it a yes or no? Sherm decided it meant yes.

"Well, if we elected her, can we unelect her now?"

"No, you can't." Trudy wiped her greasy mouth with the back of her hand. Pete winced and threw a napkin at her.

"Yes we can," Sherm said. "Because this is a democracy, and in a democracy, you can unelect people if you want to, right, Grandpa?"

"In a manner of speaking," Grandpa Marsh repeated. Then, when he saw Sherm's puzzled expression, he went on, "You can recall a person from office if that person is not doing the job."

Sherm beamed. "Good. Then I unelect you, Trudy. I recall you." It sounded so good, he said it twice.

Tip wagged his tail vigorously and barked.

"And Tip recalls you, too," Sherm added.

"Dogs can't vote," Pete objected.

"Tip is not a dog," Sherm said. "Tip is my

best friend. Friends can vote, can't they, Grandpa?"

Grandpa Marsh laughed. "In this case, I think we can make an exception for Tip. After all, he is a definite member of this family."

They looked at one another and then shouted at Trudy. "You're unelected. You've been recalled."

Trudy couldn't believe this had happened. What was so terrible about looking at TV, or missing breakfast just once, or arriving late at school? It wasn't exactly the end of the world, was it?

So Pete missed a test. Big deal. Why did he always have to be at the top of his class?

And little crybaby Sherm's teacher had been mean to him. So what? He would have a different teacher next year, wouldn't he?

And the kids in his class had laughed at him. Kids always laughed when a teacher picked on a kid, mostly because they were glad somebody else was in trouble. Tomorrow, Sherm would probably be laughing at some other poor kid who did something dumb.

When she voiced her thoughts aloud, Pete reminded her she had also neglected to order Rob to do the laundry.

"I don't believe this," Trudy exclaimed. "His name is on the list of chores Mom put up on the fridge."

Their mother had printed a schedule of chores — a day-by-day listing of what needed to be done, and who was to do what.

Heading the schedule, in bold block lettering, were the words:

NO ARGUMENTS   NO EXCUSES

Tillie reminded them, "You know what a sneak Rob is. He'll pretend he forgot."

"I'm not a sneak," Rob objected. He had to swallow a grin as he spoke, but he couldn't keep his eyes from sparkling with glee. "I did so forget."

"Sure. Accidentally on purpose," Pete told him.

"Liar. Liar. Your pants are on fire," Sherm whispered. He didn't dare say it aloud.

Trudy was furious. She pushed her chair back

so hard it fell over. She stood up and glared at them.

"You all think you're so smart. If you think you can do better, go right ahead. This was a dumb idea in the first place."

"I agree."

Trudy was surprised that Tillie agreed with her. She studied her sister. Was it possible Tillie actually liked running things? Well, that was okay with Trudy.

"Take your old job back," she said. "I don't want it."

"Not on your life," Rob said. "Tillie doesn't get her job back. We had an agreement. Now it's my turn. I'm next, remember?"

Trudy was about to leave angrily when she remembered the chocolate cake with marshmallow icing in front of Grandpa Marsh. What was she thinking of? Leave now, when it was time for dessert?

She put her chair back at the table, sat down, and asked for some cake. What she said was, "Grandpa, I'd like a real big piece of cake."

Rob looked around. His eyes began to gleam.

He rubbed his hands together. He said in a gloating voice, "I'm the boss, starting right this minute."

Tillie groaned. "From the frying pan into the fire."

6
Over My Dead Body

Sherm got a strong sinking feeling in the pit of his stomach when Tillie said that.

From the frying pan into the fire?

He shrank back in his chair. He didn't feel any better when Pete kindly explained, "Tillie means we're going from bad to worse."

Sherm understood what that meant all right. From Trudy the Moody to Rob the Slob, his least favorite person.

He pushed his food aside. Who could eat at a time when the whole world was coming to an end?

Rob didn't care what Tillie said. He looked around with a gleeful smile. No one smiled back. Tip hid behind Sherm's chair and buried his nose in his paws.

"Well," Rob said at last. "Let me think." He seemed to study each one at the table as he tried to make up his mind what to do first. Then he said, "I think it's time we all knew what Tillie writes in her diary. The one she keeps all locked up."

Every head swiveled in Tillie's direction. Grandpa Marsh frowned and was about to speak when Rob continued, "Sherm, you go up to Tillie's room and get it."

Before Sherm could protest, Tillie said, "You touch my diary and I will personally render you limb from limb."

"I'm the boss here," Rob said. "You're supposed to do what I say."

Grandpa Marsh cleared his throat noisily. "Rob," he said, after a moment. "Being boss doesn't give you the right to invade anyone's privacy."

"You better believe it, knucklehead," Tillie added. The look she gave him was as sharp as a dagger.

Rob pretended he had been joking. "I was only teasing you," he protested. "Who's interested in what a girl has to say, anyway?"

He turned his attention to Pete, who folded his arms and frowned.

"I have a great idea," Rob said. He couldn't help grinning. It wasn't just an idea, he told himself. It was a brainstorm. Now he'd get at Pete the Neat with his fussy ways. Fussy, *sissy* ways. Who ever heard of a boy like Pete? Boys were supposed to be sloppy, rough-and-tumble. Why couldn't Pete be normal, like Rob?

"Tonight I'll sleep in your room," Rob began.

Pete interrupted in a voice so cold it made Sherm shiver.

"Over my dead body," Pete answered.

"And you'll sleep in my room," Rob went on, as if he hadn't heard.

"I'd rather be strung up by my thumbs. I wouldn't sleep in your room if you paid me a million dollars. I wouldn't sleep in your room if I was dead."

"This is stupid," Trudy was annoyed. "You don't know anything about being a boss, Rob. You're supposed to tell us what to do."

"Well I was telling Tillie and Pete and they're not listening —"

"Get real, Rob," Tillie said. "You know how Mom runs the house. And how I do, too."

"Being boss isn't easy," Grandpa Marsh told Rob. "It's a responsible job. And one that requires you to be fair and just."

Rob was irritated. If he was just going to do things the way Mom and Tillie did, what fun was there in that? They all knew what their special chores were.

"Let's eat," he said. It was chicken tonight, but tomorrow, thanks to him, it would be hamburgers on thick onion rolls, piles of french fries, and loads of pickles. Rob would instruct Tillie to bring extras on everything. That was one time when she would have to obey a direct order.

Everyone was hungry, especially Tip, who couldn't understand why people yakkity-yakked when food was on the table. But when they finally ate, they did so with gusto.

Rob observed everyone around the table. He could see he would get nowhere with his sisters and brother. Grandpa Marsh didn't count. You couldn't order a grownup to do anything, especially not a grownup like Grandpa. Then his glance settled on Sherm and Tip.

Sherm, who hadn't once mentioned peanut butter and jelly, had just taken a mouthful of chicken. Suddenly he stopped chewing. He could feel Rob looking at him. He spit his food out on his plate, then fed it bit by bit to Tip.

"That dog," Rob said, "is a disgrace. Look at him slurping up your food. He must think he's died and gone to heaven. From now on," Rob insisted, "that dog does not come into the dining room when we're eating. It isn't healthy. It's dirty. Look at the way he's slobbering. Look at the floor. It's disgusting."

Everyone stopped eating to stare at Rob. *He* was disgusted? Rob? The original of all slobs?

Rob paid no attention to them.

"What's more," he went on, "from now on that dog sleeps outside in the doghouse."

"He can't do that," Sherm protested. He was afraid of Rob, but this was Tip Rob was talking about. "Tip can't sleep in a doghouse. He likes to sleep with me. He likes to sleep in my bed."

"Too bad about what Tip likes. It's time Tip

was treated like an animal and not like a human being."

"I think," Grandpa Marsh began, but Rob interrupted.

"It's not healthy, Grandpa. You know that. Dogs pick up all kind of dirt outside —"

"Tip doesn't pick up dirt. He's not like other dogs," Sherm found the courage to argue.

"That dog goes out now. I have spoken." Rob liked the sound of that so much, he repeated it. "I have spoken."

"I don't care. I won't do it." Sherm's eyes filled with tears, which he brushed away with impatience.

"Now," Rob said. "Or else."

Sherm stared at his brother. He didn't know what the or else would be, but he knew he would hate it.

Sherm stroked Tip, then said softly, "Come on, Tip. We have to go."

Usually when Sherm spoke to Tip, Tip wagged his tail. Not this time, though. Tip could recognize trouble.

"I'll get even with you, Rob. wait and see," he

muttered as he left, with Tip faithfully following.

"Put him in the doghouse and you come back and finish your supper," Rob yelled after him.

The moment Sherm left, Pete said, "You're a real prize, Rob." He threw down his napkin. "I don't want to be in the same room with you right now."

Rob knew better than to try and stop him. When Pete got tough, which wasn't often, nobody got in his way.

But Pete decided to stay.

They all seemed to have lost their appetites. No one talked to Rob or even looked at him. Finally, he couldn't stand it anymore.

"Okay, okay, if that's how you feel about it. Sherm can bring Tip back. Go get him," he told Trudy.

She immediately ran out of the room. In a moment, they heard the kitchen door slam behind her. They sat and waited. It felt like a long time, though she came racing back almost at once.

"He's gone," she cried. "Sherm is gone. And so is Tip."

7

Where's Sherm?

"I'll bet he sneaked back into the house. I'll bet he's hiding under his bed with Tip right now. You go get him, Trudy," Rob ordered.

They all knew Sherm hid under his bed during thunderstorms. Tip hid with him. He didn't know he was supposed to protect Sherm. He was a bigger coward than his master. In a storm, it was everyone for himself, Tip figured.

Sherm also hid from monsters in his closet, monsters no one else ever saw, but whom Sherm *knew* waited to leap out at him along with *things* that came out when the light went off.

That was one reason why Mrs. Evers objected to the programs Trudy always wanted to watch. She said they gave Sherm nightmares.

"He doesn't have to look," Trudy argued.

But Sherm couldn't help looking. Even when he clapped his hands over his eyes, he peered from behind them to watch.

"Those programs are giving Sherm a complex," Mrs. Evers said. "I forbid you to turn them on."

So Trudy didn't watch when her mother was home. But Mrs. Evers was gone most of the time. So the horror shows went on, since no one else objected.

Sherm was proud of the word "complex." It sounded important. If anyone called him a scaredy-cat, he would say proudly, "I have a complex."

"And I looked in the closet, too," Trudy went on. "He's not in his room. And Tip isn't, either."

"He's probably hiding in the attic," Rob said. "Pete, you go find him."

Pete didn't move.

"I gave you an order," Rob said.

"Sherm wouldn't go up to the attic, especially at night. He wouldn't go up there even if we all went up with him. I'm not wasting my time on a wild-goose chase."

"I'll go." Tillie leaped to her feet. "Maybe just this one time . . ." Her voice sounded tearful. It worried her that Sherm might be huddled somewhere, frightened but stubbornly protecting his best friend Tip.

The moment she left the room, Pete pushed back his chair. "I know he isn't there, but I'll look around in the basement."

Grandpa Marsh stood up. "He probably headed for the garage. That's the most logical place for him to go."

He left the room without a glance at Rob, who now was obviously worried.

"You and your bright ideas," Trudy said. "Why do you always pick on Sherm, anyway?"

Rob refused to answer.

Before long, Tillie was back. When Trudy and Rob looked at her, she just shrugged.

Pete had shoved boxes around in the basement, had peered behind old discarded chairs and a moth-eaten sofa, and found nothing but dust and shredded rags.

Grandpa Marsh returned, shrugging his shoulders.

Everyone was silent.

Finally, Rob stood up. He didn't look at anyone, just announced, with his head tipped toward the ceiling, "I think I'll take a look around outside."

Everyone else leaped up as well.

"I'll look up the street," Trudy said.

"And I'll look down," Pete told them. "He won't have gone far. He's too afraid of the dark to do that."

When they left, Tillie began to pace restlessly. At last she said, "I'm going to get in the car and scout around. I shouldn't have any trouble finding him."

Grandpa Marsh nodded. "I'm going back to the garage. I'll leave the door wide open so Sherm will know I'm there, waiting for him." He left, but came back quickly to say, "Leave the front door unlocked, Tillie. Just in case Sherm comes back and no one is here to let him in."

When Grandpa Marsh lifted the garage door, he turned on the lamp he used when working on his toys. It sent a warm beam into the darkness. He picked up a giraffe and began to polish it. As he polished, he whistled.

If Sherm was hiding nearby, maybe he would be tempted to come into the garage.

Twice Grandpa Marsh stopped polishing the giraffe and listened hard. Hadn't that been a small, scuffling sound? Hadn't Tip started to bark, just a quick, stifled bark, as if a hand had been clapped over his mouth?

Grandpa Marsh was tempted to walk out of the garage and call out softly, "Is that you, Sherm?"

But after a moment, he began to work on the giraffe again. He didn't want to frighten Sherm away. When Sherm was ready, he would come of his own free will.

There seemed to be no end to the waiting. He heard his grandchildren as they came back from their search. He could tell from the way they greeted each other that their search had been unsuccessful.

He thought about joining them but decided to wait. After a long while, when he had almost given up hope, he heard that small, scuffling sound again. He pretended to be absorbed in the toy in his hand. Then he said aloud, as if talking to himself, "I don't know. It just doesn't seem the same, not having Sherm here when I'm working. If he doesn't show up soon, I guess I'll have to stop. I don't know what those kids in the hospital will do. But I just can't work without Sherm."

He placed the giraffe back carefully on a shelf.

"Might as well put this light out, I guess. No use standing here and talking to myself."

Then he heard the sound again, much closer. He waited again, then said, "Well, I might as well close up shop."

"Grandpa," Sherm whispered.

"That you, Sherm?" Grandpa Marsh called.

Sherm shuffled in, head down, Tip at his side. When he raised his head, Grandpa Marsh could tell Sherm had cried a lot.

"You gave us a little bit of a scare, Sherm," Grandpa Marsh said gently. "We thought you'd run away. Where have you been?"

"Under the porch."

"It was kind of a squeeze, wasn't it? For you and Tip?"

Sherm nodded. "We wanted to run away but

we didn't know where to go. Then Tip ran in under the porch so I followed him."

"Tell you what, Sherm. Wash your face and hands and let me brush you off a little. Then why don't we go back in and talk things over. Is it a deal?"

Sherm shook his head. "No. I don't want to."

Tip barked.

"He doesn't want to, either. We're not going to talk to Rob ever again."

"You could talk to the others —"

"No. They're not my friends either. They let Rob pick on me." Sherm gave his grandfather an inquiring look, as if he wanted to ask a favor but wasn't sure his grandfather would approve.

"You have something on your mind?" Grandpa Marsh wondered. "Something special?"

"Can you help me make a sign?"

Grandpa Marsh was puzzled. "Make a sign? Now? What kind of a sign?"

"I can't tell you, Grandpa. Not until we make it, okay? I'll need two boards. One to push into the ground. And one going across for the sign."

"I think we can manage that, Sherm." Grandpa Marsh found two boards that seemed just right for a sign.

"I need something to write with, Grandpa."

"I have this marking crayon," Grandpa said. "You want me to write down what you want to put on it?"

"No. I have to do it myself."

"Okay. Mind if I watch?"

"Are you going to tell me not to say what I'm going to say?" Sherm sent his grandfather an anxious look.

Grandpa Marsh shook his head. "This is a free country, Sherm. Write away. I won't even look if you don't want me to."

"You can look when I'm finished." Sherm pressed down hard on the crayon. He wanted his message to be very clear. While he wrote, the tip of his tongue popped out from one corner of his lips to another. He always did that when he concentrated.

"You can look now if you want to," he said at last.

Grandpa Marsh's eyes twinkled when he read Sherm's sign. Then he said, sounding quite serious, "You sure you want to say this, Sherm? Wouldn't you like to talk it over a little bit first?"

Sherm shook his head. "No."

He had what Trudy called his "mulish" look. His grandfather knew nothing he could say now would change Sherm's mind.

"Will you help me hammer it down in the lawn out front, Grandpa? Near the porch where the light will shine on it? So anybody going by can read it?"

"If that's what you really want. Then I suggest we go back to the house, Sherm. You know your sisters and brothers are really worried about you."

"No, they're not. They're not my friends."

Grandpa Marsh decided not to try to change Sherm's mind just now.

"Okay, Sherm. Show me where you want the sign and I'll set it up for you."

He knew that the others waiting in the house would be angry when they read the sign, but he couldn't help thinking they deserved to be shaken up a little.

"You're not going to tell them, are you?" Sherm was afraid someone would rush out and knock the sign down.

"My word of honor," Grandpa Marsh said. He smiled to himself. Nothing would come of this sign, of course, but if it helped Sherm get rid of some of his anger, it was worthwhile.

Sherm watch anxiously as his grandfather hammered the sign into the firm ground out front.

"There. That will hold," Grandpa Marsh said finally.

Sherm believed his grandfather, but he tested it anyway. Yes, he thought as he tugged at it, it would hold, even in a strong wind.

"Can we go into the house now?" Grandpa Marsh asked. "They're mighty worried about you."

"About me?" Sherm asked in disbelief. He shook his head, but he put his hand in his grandfather's. Tip walked quietly beside them.

Neither one looked back at the sign, which read:

FAMILY FOR SALE
(except my dog Tip)

8

Pete's Plan

When Grandpa Marsh and Sherm walked into the dining room, everyone talked at once.

"Sherm!" Tillie's voice sounded as if she had swallowed a throatful of tears. "You scared us half to death. Where were you?"

At the same time, Trudy began to scold him. "Don't you ever do a dumb thing like that again. You ought to be ashamed of yourself, running off in the dark like that."

Pete just shook his head, but his smile was broad with relief.

Rob was angry. He yelled, "You don't have the sense you were born with. Where did you think you were going?"

Sherm glanced around in surprise. He couldn't believe how upset and worried they had been. They really did care about him after all! He turned to Rob. "You told me to put Tip in the doghouse."

"So?" Rob asked impatiently. "You put Tip in the doghouse —"

Sherm shook his head. "Tip didn't want to go in the doghouse."

"*Tip* didn't want to go into the doghouse?" Rob clapped his hands to his head in exasperation. "I suppose he told you that? Just up and said, 'Sherm, I'm not going into that doghouse. No way.'" He sighed. "Listen, dummy —"

Tillie turned on her brother angrily. "Don't you dare call him names. Just leave him alone, hear?"

"Well, where were you?" Pete wanted to know. "We looked everywhere."

"In the crawlspace. Under the front porch. Tip didn't want to walk around in the dark. He got scared. So he ran into the crawlspace."

"And of course you had to squeeze in there, too, right?" Rob asked. "You thought that was real smart?"

"Yes, it was," Sherm said, defiantly. "Tip always

sleeps with me, especially when I'm scared. Well, Tip was scared, so it was my turn to stay with him."

"Why don't we let the matter rest?" Grandpa Marsh suggested. "Sherm is okay. We haven't had dessert. It would be a shame to let it go to waste."

Pete gave his grandfather a small, knowing smile. "I've never seen dessert go to waste in this house, Grandpa. Let's give Sherm the first serving, as a welcome home gift."

"Next time I give somebody an order," Rob mumbled through a large mouthful of cake, "I expect —"

Pete interrupted. "There isn't gong to be a next time. I'm taking over, Rob. You think being the boss is making everyone miserable. I think we've been going about this all wrong. Grandpa was right."

Everyone turned to stare at Grandpa Marsh.

"Right about what?" Trudy wanted to know.

"Right about the responsibilities that go with being a boss. Seems to me everybody is always telling somebody what to do. Like Mom putting the list on the fridge. Like Tillie trying her best to be like Mom. Let me finish," he said as Tillie tried to interrupt.

Pete studied his brothers and sisters thoughtfully for a moment, then went on. "It's real hard on Mom, working the way she does, then rushing off to school at night."

"Why does she do that?" Sherm asked. "Why can't she just stay home and be a regular mom?"

"You think she wants to be a waitress all her life?" Trudy asked. "She wants to make something of herself, be somebody."

Grandpa Marsh nodded. "You're right, Trudy. Does everyone understand she wants it for all of you as much as for herself?"

"And we haven't helped her one bit," Pete continued. "Always complaining. Always thinking how hard things are for us. The things we have to do around the house. Well, I've got some ideas about that."

"You would," Rob said. "You're Mr. Smarty Pants."

"I've come up with a better plan than Mom's. Mom decides what she wants us to do. We all hate the jobs she assigns to us," Pete went on, ignoring his brother. "I think we should decide which jobs we would rather do. And another thing — why can't we work as teams? That way each job would take half the time."

Tillie looked interested. "Like how?" she asked.

"Trudy," Pete said, "which job do you hate most?"

"Doing the laundry," she said promptly. "It takes forever. And it's boring. Boring, boring, boring."

"I hate the vacuuming. And the dusting. And picking up stuff from the furniture," Rob said.

"Suppose we divide up each job," Pete suggested. "Suppose one person puts the laundry in the washer. And another one takes it out and puts it in the dryer. And somebody else takes it out of the dryer and has somebody else help fold it and put it all away?"

Trudy brightened. "I could go for that," she agreed.

"I could help put away stuff in everybody's dresser," Sherm offered.

Grandpa Marsh remained quiet, but they could see that he approved of Pete's idea.

"We could do that with everything we have to do," Pete went on.

"Like I could vacuum the living room," Trudy said.

"And I could vacuum the upstairs hall and one bedroom," Tillie agreed.

"And each week we could switch jobs so no-body is stuck with one chore all the time," Pete said. "Are you with me?"

"Yes," Tillie agreed at once.

"You bet," said Trudy.

Rob remained silent.

"And anybody who doesn't want to do his share," Pete said, glaring at Rob, "would find no one would talk to him, or have anything to do with him. Just treat him like he didn't exist."

"Starting now," Tillie said, giving her brother a frosty glance.

Rob shrugged. He turned to his grandfather. "There's some cake left over. You might as well give it to me, Grandpa."

Grandpa Marsh made no move to put the last bit of cake on the plate Rob held out. He didn't speak, either.

Pete rose to clear the dishes. Trudy jumped up to help him. Sherm carried his plate into the kitchen. Tillie began brushing crumbs from the table into a small dustpan. No one spoke. No one looked at Rob.

Rob sat with folded arms, his mouth a stubborn line of anger. But after a while, he couldn't stand being ignored.

Without a word, he went into the kitchen and began stacking some of the dishes in the dishwasher.

Pete winked at Sherm, who stared open-mouthed at the sight of Rob doing something he hadn't been ordered and yelled at to do.

"You know what," Pete said, after the dining room was clean and ready for breakfast the following morning. "We can sleep later tomorrow because we don't have school on Saturday. Let's have a meeting after breakfast and decide who wants to do what. Then we can make up a new schedule to put up on the fridge, so nobody will forget what each one of us is supposed to do from now on. Agreed?"

"Agreed," they said, even Rob.

"Well," Grandpa Marsh said, before leaving to go back to his own apartment. "This has been a day of surprises. Who knows what kind of surprise we're in for next?"

Even Grandpa Marsh couldn't imagine the surprise that awaited them the next morning.

9

If It's Broken, Don't Nix It

The next morning, even though it was not a school day, everyone showed up for breakfast at the same time.

Rob waited to say what he thought until breakfast was over, the dishes cleared away, and the meeting about to start.

That's what Pete called it — the meeting. He said, "I call this meeting to order."

"I changed my mind," Rob announced.

"Big surprise," Trudy said. "You afraid you might have to do some work for a change?"

Rob ignored her. "I just don't want anybody telling me what to do and when to do it, that's all."

"Nobody is crazy about doing chores," Pete said.

71

"You are," Rob shot back.

"Grow up, Rob." Tillie sounded impatient. "You might as well get used to the idea that everybody has to do things they don't like once in a while. You think Mom enjoys running herself ragged, working all day, going to school at night? You think any of us like doing all these boring chores? What's the use of complaining? It doesn't make things any easier, does it?"

"Well —" Rob began but stopped when Tillie rushed on.

"Get this through your head. Nobody here is going to let you sit around while the rest of us do the work."

"You tell him, Tillie." Trudy clasped her hands and waved them over her head.

"No more pretending you've forgotten what you're supposed to do, either," Pete added.

"Amen to that," Tillie said. The smile she gave Rob made him scrunch down in his seat.

Sherm had only half-listened to the others. He had been thinking. He wanted to show them all that he could be smart and helpful. So when everyone fell silent for the moment, he said, "I have an idea for the meeting."

Everyone looked at him in surprise.

Rob couldn't help it: "Pipe down, Sherm," he said. "Nobody wants to hear it."

"Let him talk," Grandpa Marsh told Rob. He said it very quietly, but there was steel in his voice.

"Last time I looked," Tillie said, "Sherm was a member of this family. He has as much right to talk as the rest of us. And don't you forget that, Rob." She turned and looked at the others. "Don't any of you forget it."

"You bet," Trudy said, and flashed a warm smile at Sherm.

"That gets my vote," Pete said.

Sherm was startled. When had they become his friends? Maybe they really had been worried when they couldn't find him. Maybe they had even been scared they might not ever be able to find him.

He thought about the sign Grandpa Marsh had helped him make. Last night it had seemed the perfect solution. This morning, finding out they cared about him, listening to them telling Rob off, he changed his mind. Maybe later, while they were doing the chores, he could ask

Grandpa Marsh to help him pull the sign out and throw it away.

"Sherm," Tillie interrupted his thoughts. "You said you had an idea. We're waiting to hear it, okay?"

"I was thinking," Sherm began, looking away so he wouldn't see Rob's face, "that instead of everybody picking and choosing and then arguing, why don't we put the different jobs down on little pieces of paper. Then we could throw them in the breadbasket and everybody can pull out one piece of paper and has to do the job it says to do."

Pete spoke up quickly. "That's brilliant, Sherm. I vote for that."

"Me, too," Trudy agreed.

Tillie leaned over and kissed Sherm on the cheek. He brushed it off quickly. Why did his sister do that? It was embarrassing.

Grandpa Marsh beamed.

Pete got the breadbasket and a pad and pencil from the kitchen. He tore a sheet from the pad in strips, then began to write. His handwriting, like everything else about Pete, was very neat. In a few moments, he threw the strips into the basket, then stirred them round and round.

"Who wants to go first?" he asked.

Every hand shot up, except Grandpa Marsh's, of course. Rob held up his hand because he was afraid if he went last, his strip of paper would list a chore he especially hated.

Just as Rob began to shove aside the other reaching hands, the doorbell rang. Everyone was startled. Who could be ringing the bell at eight o'clock on a Saturday morning?

There was a chorus of "I'll get it"s from Trudy, Rob, and Pete, but Tillie told them all to stay put. She was out of her chair and on her way to the front door in seconds. Tip went along. He did not take kindly to strangers. Strangers didn't know, of course, that though Tip was big and his bark ferocious, he was a natural-born coward who would hide if you yelled "boo" at him.

When Tillie swung the door open, Tip roared like a lion until he saw who it was. Then he wagged his tail and waited to be petted.

"What a watchdog," the man at the door said.

"You scared even me, and we're old friends, right, Tip?"

"Mr. Fixit," Tillie said, surprised. "Is the microwave oven fixed already?" She peered down at the step to see if he had placed it there.

"Ready?" the man laughed. "I'm fast, but I'm not a miracle worker."

The man standing in the doorway was about Tillie's height. The gray hair that curled around his head seemed to run down into his short gray beard. A small bushy gray mustache almost hid his upper lip. His eyes were a bright, merry brown, even when he was serious. He wore washed-out jeans of no special color and a T-shirt that said:

if it's broken, don't nix it
just bring it to me, your friend Mr. Fixit

Tillie was puzzled. Mrs. Evers brought small appliances to Mr. Fixit from time to time but he didn't usually deliver repair work.

Not knowing what to say, she spoke the first words that sprang to mind.

"Mom's not here. She's away on a cruise."

"I know. She told me she won a cruise. Good for her. She needs a vacation. No," he went on, as Tillie waited, "I was just passing on my way to the shop."

Tillie nodded. Mr. Fixit lived on the next block. He regularly went by on his way to and from work.

"I came about the sign."

"Sign? What sign?"

Why was Mr. Fixit acting in this odd way, Tillie wondered. She soon found out.

"The sign you had on your front lawn. See?"

He had held it behind him. Now he turned it right side up and showed it to her.

Tillie's jaw dropped. Then her face flushed, and her eyes flashed with anger. She was about to explode when Grandpa Marsh came and stood beside her.

"I think," Grandpa Marsh said, "you'd better come in."

"Grandpa," Tillie said, "I'd like to know whose big idea that was, putting up a sign like this. Sherm wrote it, didn't he? I know his handwriting."

"Let's go into the dining room," her grandfather insisted. "Everything can be explained better when we're sitting down together . . ."

"Listen," Mr. Fixit said. "I'd better get going. I shouldn't have disturbed you, but the sign bothered me . . ." His voice trailed off. "It seemed to me maybe somebody here was hurting, am I right?"

"You're not disturbing us," Grandpa Marsh told him. "You've known our family a long time. Come in. Come in."

Mr. Fixit followed Grandpa Marsh. He whispered to Tillie, "I must admit I'm very curious. You don't come across a For Sale sign like this one on a front lawn very often." He chuckled. "What am I saying? You don't come across a sign like this in a million years."

The moment the three came into the dining room, Sherm slid down in his chair. He wished there were some magic words that would make him invisible. Tip seemed to understand exactly how Sherm felt, for he put a paw on Sherm's arm and gave him a pleading look, as if to say, "Let's get out of here."

The others stared at Mr. Fixit, and the sign he still held.

"Are you advertising something?" Trudy asked. No one could see the words yet, for Mr. Fixit had held the sign down when he entered the room.

"Not me," Mr. Fixit said.

Pete pulled out a chair so Mr. Fixit could sit down. "Does it have something to do with your shop?" he asked.

"Listen, folks," Mr. Fixit said. "Maybe I shouldn't be here at all. It's just that I know your mom, such a fine lady, so hard working . . ." He stopped talking. "Listen," he began again, "I know it's none of my business, but I just couldn't pass by that sign —"

"You keep talking about the sign," Rob broke in. "What does it say and why don't you show it to us?"

Trudy and Pete seemed about to burst with questions as well.

Mr. Fixit looked helplessly at Grandpa Marsh.

"You may as well hold it up for them to see," he suggested.

Sherm swallowed hard. "I think Tip has to go out now," he said. "I better take him out."

"Not so fast, Sherm," Tillie said. The look she gave him made Sherm squirm. No doubt about it. Tillie knew who wrote that sign. And she wasn't happy about it. Her lips were pressed together hard, as if she didn't want angry words to escape.

Mr. Fixit fussed with the sign, pretending he was having a hard time turning it right-side up. When he had it up where everyone could read it, he sighed.

10

Family for Sale?

They all knew at once it was Sherm's sign.

"Family for sale?" Pete said. "*This* family? For *sale?*"

Every eye was on Sherm now.

"I don't believe this." Trudy stared at Sherm. "You actually wanted to *sell* us? Your own family?"

"Cute," Rob said. "That's really cute. what were you going to ask for us? A million dollars?"

"I'd better go now," Mr. Fixit said, but he couldn't seem to bring himself to get up and leave. He couldn't help being curious either, and sorry as well, for he liked this family. Their mother was one of his best customers. She always found time to chat with him, no matter how rushed she was.

The others paid no attention to him.

"I can't understand you, Sherm. Why would you even think of such a thing?" Tillie asked.

Sherm glanced at his grandfather, wanting him to help, but Grandpa Marsh just folded his arms and waited.

"Okay. I'll tell you why. It's because I don't like you anymore. You and Trudy and Pete. But I hate Rob —"

"Hey, wait a minute," Rob protested. "You can't say that. I'm your brother."

Sherm turned and faced Rob with so fiery a stare that Rob drew back in his chair. It was an awful feeling. He knew the others didn't like him very much, but they got along fairly well, even so. At least he thought so.

"I don't want you to be my brother anymore," Sherm told him.

"Okay, so you don't like Rob," Tillie broke in. "But I can't believe you don't like me —"

"Or me," Pete put in quickly.

"Yeah. And why me?" Trudy wanted to know.

At first it seemed Sherm wouldn't explain to anyone; then Grandpa Marsh said, "You might as well get this all out in the open, Sherm."

"Start with me," Tillie ordered. "How can you not like me? You know I'm a responsible, caring sister."

"No, you're not. Whenever Rob picks on me, and he always picks on me . . ."

Every head swiveled toward Rob.

Every eye was cold.

Rob looked away.

Sherm had stopped speaking.

"Go on," Tillie urged. "I want to hear this."

"Whenever I tried to tell you how mean Rob was to me, you'd say, 'Not now, Sherm,' or 'I'm busy, Sherm,' or you'd wave your hand at me and say 'It'll have to wait till later, Sherm' or 'Just don't pay attention to Rob,' or —"

Tillie told Sherm hastily, "Okay, okay. I get the message."

"See?" Sherm said. "You're doing it again. That's what you always do."

"Well, I've never been too busy to talk to you, Sherm." Trudy sounded smug. "I never put you off like that."

"Yes, you did," Sherm contradicted her. "Whenever I tried to talk to you, you always said, 'I can't be bothered now, Sherm — here come the walking dead,' or 'Later, Sherm, this part is where the aliens make the space pilots walk through the slime pits' or —"

"Well, you always wanted to talk just at the most interesting parts," Trudy explained.

Pete stared at his sisters. "What a rotten thing to do, when all Sherm wanted —"

"You weren't any help, either," Sherm accused Pete. "You always told me I had to learn to fight my own battles. You always said —"

Pete broke in hastily.

"I was just trying to get you to have more fight in you," he said. "You know, more backbone —"

"I'm only eight years old," Sherm reminded him. "Eight-year-old kids don't have backbone when someone bigger and meaner and stronger is picking on them."

There was silence. Tillie looked down at the table; Pete fiddled with the strips of paper in the breadbasket; Rob stared up at the ceiling as if he had never noticed it before.

Mr. Fixit cleared his throat. He started to rise from his chair. "Listen," he said. "This is a family affair. A stranger like me, well, I'm no stranger exactly, but an outsider. Yes, that's better. An outsider has no business here right now."

"Wait," Tillie said.

Mr. Fixit sat down again, but on the edge of his chair, so he could get up quickly if he had to.

"Did anything like this ever happen in your family, Mr. Fixit?" she asked.

"You mean when I was growing up?" he asked. When she nodded, he said, "I didn't have a family when I was a kid."

"Yes, you did," Sherm protested. "Everybody has a family —"

Mr. Fixit interrupted. "No, Sherm. You'd be surprised how many orphans there are, or abandoned kids. I was brought up in an orphanage. I was left there on the doorstep when I was a baby. I never knew who my parents were. I don't to this day. Even my name isn't my real name."

"That's awful," Tillie said. "What a terrible thing to do to a baby."

Trudy stared at Mr. Fixit as if she couldn't believe what she had just heard. "You mean somebody really just dumped you, just like that?"

Mr. Fixit shrugged. "It happens. More often than we know about."

"There must have been a note left with you," Pete said. "Something that could have been a clue."

"There was a note," Mr. Fixit began.

Pete smiled. "I figured there might be. If you still have the note — I mean, if they saved it at the orphanage — then maybe you can still track down your family."

Mr. Fixit shook his head. "That only happens in storybooks. All the note said was 'His name is Sam.' That was the whole message."

"That couldn't have been the whole message," Rob argued. "Didn't it say Sam August? That's the name on the window of your shop — *Sam August, your Mr. Fixit.* There can't be too many families named August."

"Probably not," Mr. Fixit agreed. "But it was the orphanage that gave me that name. Because I was left on the doorstep on August first." He paused, then glanced around at the others. "Listen, you don't want to hear all this."

Sherm for one wanted to hear it all, and said so. The others agreed.

"I used to dream all the time what it must be like to have parents, grandparents, and brothers and sisters. I even dreamed of having uncles and aunts and cousins by the dozens." He laughed.

"But you do have a family," Tillie said. "I've seen your wife in the shop often."

"Of course I have a family. *Now*. But not when I was growing up in the orphanage. I was a telephone repairman after I left, and not much of a talker. I was a loner. I felt like I was always on the outside looking in. Then one day I went to a house to repair a phone line, and there was the future Mrs. August." He laughed again. "I fell in love with her at once, just looking at her. Then I fell in love even more when I found out she had three sisters and two brothers. And a father and a mother. And a grandfather and a grandmother. All of a sudden, I had a real, genuine, honest-to-goodness family."

Grandpa Marsh smiled. "Let's not forget your own honest-to-goodness family — your sons and daughter."

Mr. Fixit nodded. "And now my grandchildren as well. The noise when we all get together.

The shrieks and the fighting and the bedlam —"
He grinned. "I love it."

Sherm stared at Mr. Fixit. He loved it?

"You love when your kids have fights?" he asked. "You mean when Teddy always yells 'Rickie hit me' and Rickie yells back 'he started it' and Jenny cries 'Susie grabbed my doll' and Susie screams 'it's my doll, it's my doll' . . . and on and on?"

Mr. Fixit smiled at Sherm. Then he shrugged. "Kids are kids. It takes a long time to grow up. Meanwhile, you try to understand and hope they'll all still be talking to one another when they're adults."

Sherm said, "Were you afraid they wouldn't like each other when they grew up?"

"Of course not. Brothers and sisters argue and fight. They get mad; they don't talk to each other. They make up; they're friends. They get mad again —" Mr. Fixit broke off. "Parents sometimes feel their kids are little monsters. But listen, Sherm. Show me a family where everything goes smoothly all the time, and I'll give that family a medal."

Mr. Fixit stood up. He reached for the sign, then asked, "Shall I throw this in the trash on my way out?"

"No," Grandpa Marsh said. "I have an idea about that."

No sooner had the front door closed behind Mr. Fixit when Grandpa Marsh said, "I have a feeling, Sherm, that things are going to be a little different from now on. I think your sign has made all of us take a good hard look at ourselves."

"You mean Tillie and Trudy and Pete will be my friends from now on?" Sherm asked.

"Sure," Pete told him promptly.

"Of course," Trudy agreed.

"Trust me," Tillie said.

Rob was silent. Tillie was about to tear into him when he said, "Okay, okay. I get the message."

"Let's get rid of the sign," Tillie said.

Before she could reach for it, Grandpa Marsh shook his head. "No, Tillie. I'm going to frame that sign and hang it up right here in the dining room. As a reminder. In case we forget."

11

The Lucky Sign

When they all came down to breakfast the next morning, the sign was in place. Everyone glanced at it quickly, then looked away.

For a few moments, no one spoke.

Then Rob demanded, "Do I have to sit here and stare at that sign every time we have a meal?"

"That's the whole idea," Pete told him.

"Because Sherm was giving us a message," Trudy said.

"Personally," Tillie smiled at Sherm, who was beginning to huddle in his chair, "I think it turned out to be a lucky sign."

Rob stared at her in disbelief. "Lucky? You call a sign that offers a family up for sale *lucky*?"

"Yes. I do. Because it reminded us we *are* a

family, and not just a bunch of people living together in the same house, too busy to have time for each other."

"You mean too busy for Sherm the —" Rob stopped abruptly when he saw how everyone glared at him.

"And that's another thing," Tillie went on in a frosty voice. "I think we've had enough name-calling. It stops right now —"

"Does that include me?" Rob wanted to know. "No more calling me Rob the Slob?"

"It will be hard," Tillie said. "But yes, no more calling anybody a name."

For several days, everyone was careful. Mrs. Evers would have called it 'tiptoeing on eggshells.'

"And one more item," Tillie remembered. "We agree to pay a little more attention to Sherm. Agreed?"

"Agreed," they all said solemnly.

For the most part, they did find time for Sherm. Once in a while they slipped back into the old ways. Two days later, Tillie, writing in her diary at her desk, looked up at Sherm with a far-away look in her eyes when he came into her room.

"Not now, Sherm," she told him impatiently. "I'll talk to you later."

Sherm left without a word.

"See?" he said to Tip later. "Tillie was too busy again."

Tip looked mournful.

Together they went into the living room, where Trudy was glued to the TV screen. She had finished a bag of potato chips and was now munching a chocolate bar.

"Trudy," Sherm said.

Tip helped by growling softly.

Trudy waved her hand at Sherm. "Not now, Sherm," she said. "I can't be bothered now. This is the part where the Super Mongoose turns all the kids into green frogs with bulging eyes and . . ."

Sherm didn't wait to hear the rest.

He looked at Tip and shrugged his shoulders.

"She can't be bothered now," Sherm said. "Let's go find Pete."

Pete had locked his door. That meant he was cramming for an important test, and if you disturbed him, you were taking your life in your hands.

Sherm didn't know exactly what that meant, but he wasn't about to try to find out.

The reason Sherm had tried to reach out to his sisters and brother was the usual one. Rob had ordered him to go to his room to find his cap — the one that had printed on it in large black letters I TAKE NO PRISONERS.

With a deep sigh, Sherm had dragged himself up the steps to Rob's room. When he found the cap after a desperate search, he went back to the dining room, where Rob worked on his model plane, and threw it on the table. Sherm ran out before Rob could think of some other errand for him to run.

That evening, when they were all having supper, Rob suddenly told Sherm, "I left my cap in the living room. Go get it."

"You just wait a minute," Tillie told Rob, but stopped because Sherm had stood up so fast and hard, his chair fell over. He looked at all of them, letting his glance move from Tillie to Trudy to Pete. When it came to Grandpa Marsh, Sherm took a deep breath. Grandpa Marsh gave Sherm an encouraging nod, almost as if he knew what would happen next.

"No, you wait, Tillie," Sherm said. Then he turned to Rob. "You want your cap? Go get it yourself."

Then, trembling, he waited for the sky to fall.

"Why, you little worm," Rob exploded. "You can't talk to me like that —"

"Yes I can," Sherm broke in. "I said no — N-O — and I mean it. I'm not going to let you scare me anymore. Even if you hit me . . ."

Tip stood up, put his paws on the table, and growled at Rob, a mean, threatening sound that made Rob push back against his chair.

"What's the matter with him?" Rob asked. "Don't you growl at me, Tip, if you know what's good for you."

"Tip is saying NO, too," Sherm pointed out.

Pete applauded. "Good for you. See? You do have backbone, just what I've been telling you all along."

Tillie reached over and patted Sherm on the back.

"I think writing that sign was your declaration of independence. Congratulations, Sherm."

Sherm wasn't sure what that meant, but he was pleased.

"Way to go, Sherm," Trudy said.

Sherm was pleased with himself.

Rob looked stunned.

"And I'm never ever going to let you order me around anymore, or call me names. Not ever," Sherm added.

Later, back in his room, with Tip's head in his lap so Sherm could stroke him, Sherm said, "You know something, Tip?"

Tip raised his head and looked into Sherm's eyes earnestly.

"That's what I like about you, Tip. You're never too busy, or don't want to be bothered, or anything."

Tip licked Sherm's face.

"You know something else?" Sherm went on. "I think Tillie was right. That sign I made? It did turn out to be a lucky sign. Because it was like Tillie said, my declaration of independence."

That was a big mouthful of words for Sherm, but he figured they were the best words in the English language.

J   Clifford, Eth, 1915-
CLI
      Family for sale

      DATE DUE

HIC *   JUN -- 1996

Discarded
         Co. Public Lib
Blue Grass Regional Library
Columbia, Tennessee 38401